THE GAME

THE DO-OVER

THE GAME

ELIZABETH NEAL

darbycreek

MINNEAPOLIS

Darby Creek
A division of Lerner Publishing Group, Inc.
241 First Avenue North
Minneapolis, MN 55401 USA

For reading levels and more information, look up this title at www.lernerbooks.com.

Image credits: MPIX/Shutterstock.com; VshenZ/Shutterstock.com.

Main body text set in Janson Text LT Std 12/17.5.
Typeface provided by Adobe Systems.

Library of Congress Cataloging-in-Publication Data

Names: Neal, Elizabeth, 1970– author.
Title: The game / Elizabeth Neal.
Description: Minneapolis : Darby Creek, [2019] | Series: The do-over | Summary:
    High school senior Marcus makes a mistake in an important basketball game, but
    will the mysterious gift of a chance to relive the day make things better or worse?
Identifiers: LCCN 2018019471 (print) | LCCN 2018036292 (ebook) |
    ISBN 9781541541948 (eb pdf) | ISBN 9781541540316 (lb : alk. paper) |
    ISBN 9781541545502 (pb : alk. paper)
Subjects: | CYAC: Basketball—Fiction. | Best friends—Fiction. | Friendship—
    Fiction. | High schools—Fiction. | Schools—Fiction. | Conduct of life—Fiction.
Classification: LCC PZ7.1.N379 (ebook) | LCC PZ7.1.N379 Gam 2019 (print) |
    DDC [Fic]—dc23

LC record available at https://lccn.loc.gov/2018019471

Manufactured in the United States of America
1-45236-36618-8/13/2018

FOR JOHN AND MAGGIE

1

"Marcus, put your phone away, man!" Taj whacked him on the head. "We're gonna be late for basketball practice."

Marcus shrugged him off without looking up. "Taj, you worry too much. We've got, like . . . eight minutes."

Taj jumped up and tried to tag the chains that hung from the basketball hoop Marcus was leaning against. He was taller than Marcus but not great at getting off the ground. He came up several inches short, but the dude kept on trying. Marcus had to give him that.

Marcus knew why Taj was freaking out. Tomorrow was the last game of their regular season. Honestly, he was nervous too. It could be the last chance they would ever have to see some court time. He and Taj had been dreaming of making the starting five since way back in middle school, when they first started playing basketball together.

But realistically, Marcus knew the chances of them even playing were low. For one thing, he was only five foot six. In middle school, that had seemed so tall, but then everybody else kept growing.

He was fast, at least, and had a pretty good outside shot. But Coach Hunter kept telling Marcus that if he wanted to play he needed to work on his passing game. And his ball-handling skills. And spotting the open players. Okay, he had some things he still needed to work on. And Marcus had been working on them—he really had. But would his work pay off?

Taj said, "Come on, man. We've got to go."

"Wait, just give me one more minute," Marcus said. "I'm about to win this thing. I'm using my trivia powers for good here."

He tapped the button for the answer he knew was right.

But his phone played a different tune than he expected: a sad *womp-womp-wahhh*. His on-screen character's eyes turned to *X*'s.

Marcus groaned as he pushed himself off the cold, cracked playground. "All right, let's head in." A message popped up on his phone:

> Congratulations! That's your personal best!
> You've earned an extra life for next time.
> Bank it or play?

"Coach Hunter's going to make us do fifty stair laps if we're late." Taj hopped from foot to foot, stretching his arms behind his head. "If you make him mad today, we're never going to get any playing time."

The Booker T. Washington Wolves were 11 for 14 this season and had a good chance to make it to Districts for the first time in almost ten years. Coach Hunter was hyped and had been working them extra hard the last couple practices. Marcus had to be honest—it was kind of exciting. When he didn't let his nerves get in the way, he had a decent three-pointer. Maybe today would be his lucky day. He just had to show Coach that he could run the plays too.

He selected "Bank it" and followed Taj into the side entrance of the school.

The locker room smelled like sweat and bleach, but Marcus didn't mind. He just needed to get changed and he'd be in the gym. The gym always felt like home somehow. He knew exactly what he was supposed to be doing there. Marcus could hear basketballs thumping, then clanging off the metal rims, and the squeak of sneakers changing direction on the old wooden floors.

He changed quickly into workout clothes and threw his stuff into a locker that popped open again every time he tried to shut it. He didn't even bother trying to lock it—the door was too crooked to close properly. Everything in their school was so old it barely worked.

Marcus and Taj ran onto the court just in time to avoid stair laps. Coach Hunter was blowing his whistle. He started them out with the usual warm-up: five laps around the court. Marcus felt his limbs loosen up as he trotted around the ancient gym. It felt good to move.

He loved this sport so much, but to be totally real, it didn't always love him back. He and Taj had been playing together since seventh grade without ever making the starting lineup. That was how they had become best friends. It was a bonding experience, being in the middle of the pack together.

They weren't terrible. But nobody was lining up to shower them with scholarship money. Still, somebody had to keep the starting players on their toes at practice. Though they weren't the strongest players, they worked hard and they loved the game. Honestly, they had to love it to keep at it after years of riding the bench.

He and Taj were seniors now. The season was coming to an end. They were going in different directions after high school, so this would be their last year of playing on a team together. They'd been working their butts off all year, but some of the other players on the team were seriously gifted. If Marcus ever wanted to get some playing time, he'd have to take it up a notch today.

Coach Hunter whistled again and clapped his hands together. He was a short, intense older man who always warned the kids never to take up smoking. He had quit years ago but had never managed to kick the chewing gum habit that had replaced the cigarettes. He kept a pack of mint gum in his shirt pocket at all times. Marcus was impressed that somebody so cranky could have such great-smelling breath.

Coach led them through a series of hamstring stretches, then went to the rack for a couple of basketballs.

"All right, guys, gather up. Two lines." The players took their places at the top of the free throw lane—one line for shooting layups, the other for rebounding. Marcus and Taj hustled to get to the front of the layup line to impress Coach.

Coach held one ball on his hip and dribbled the other ball fast and low to get their attention. "We're going to start with left-handed layups today." Everyone groaned and laughed—they were almost all right-handed. *Why does Coach have to start with the harder side?* Marcus thought.

Coach Hunter bounced one ball to Marcus and the other to Taj, who was right behind him. Marcus tried to focus. The left was definitely his weak side, but it was just a layup. He took off for the basket, but he couldn't relax. His rhythm was all wrong. He came in fast and put it up a little too hard. *Clang.* His shot bounced off the rim. Marcus winced. Great start.

Taj was coming in right behind him. His layup went in, but as he came down he tripped over his shoelace and went sprawling out of bounds. Marcus doubled back to help him up, bringing him into a chest bump. "Yes! Misfits unite." They laughed, a little embarrassed.

Julio scooped up the rebound and passed it back to the player in the shooting line. "Hey, at least it went in. Doesn't have to be pretty." He gave Taj a low five.

Julio was the starting point guard. He was killing it this season, making plays happen when nobody thought it was even possible. He wasn't much taller than Marcus, but he had an uncanny sense for where people were going to move next. Marcus always joked that Julio was low-key psychic. It seemed like he always knew where the ball was heading before the other players knew themselves.

Julio circled around to get back in line on the other side. Marcus raised his eyebrows and pointed down at Taj's feet. He put on a gentle kindergarten-teacher voice. "Do you need help tying your shoes?"

"Dude, shut up." Taj grinned and fixed his laces.

Marcus would miss hanging out with him next year.

"All right, power layups now!" Coach called out after the whole team had cycled through the first exercise. "Work on a nice clean jump stop. Imagine you've got a defender right behind you. You want to stop short and let him fly by. Then lay it right into the basket."

Taj grinned. Power layups were his favorite shot. This time he crushed it.

After the whole team had shot from both sides, Coach Hunter called everybody over for a pep talk. Coach popped a fresh piece of gum out of his pack and got it going before he addressed the team.

"Okay, guys. Tomorrow's the last big game of the season! This one will determine if our season is over or if we go on to the districts."

Marcus nudged Taj in the ribs and muttered, "Yeah, can't wait to go out in glory—riding the bench!"

Taj laughed. "We're going to sit on that bench like we've never sat before!" Behind the cover of their taller teammates, they gave each other their elaborate handshake routine: dap, double-slap, finger-hook, hand explosion.

Somehow, Coach Hunter spotted them and shot them a warning look. Then he went on, "Next up is the three-second box-out drill. Put the ball on the ground, right there on the free-throw line. I want you to make contact with your opponent, then turn to box out."

The players all started to move into position, and Coach barked, "Not yet! Eyes on me. Your goal is to keep the offensive player from getting to the ball within three seconds. Keep your base low, get your arms out. No fouls, okay? Keep it clean."

Marcus gave Taj a nod. They had heard these instructions a million times and knew what was coming next. Coach Hunter was a little bit obsessed with rebounding. He smacked his clipboard and pointed at the players.

"Teams that grab the most rebounds get twice as many chances to score, right? So long as we keep control of that ball, we get to keep shooting. And the more you put it up, the better your chances one of those shots goes in. So let's see some hustle today. Now move!"

They broke out of the huddle and got in line for the drill. Marcus lowered his voice to do his best impression of Coach, with his own special spin. He looked at Taj, worked his jaw like he was chewing gum, and pointed over to the sidelines. "So long as we keep sitting on that bench, the warmer it gets. The warmer it gets, the better our chances the school will one day recognize our greatness and engrave our names onto a commemorative bench."

Taj snorted. He whispered back, "Man, don't let Coach hear you. We'll never get to play if we tick him off!"

Marcus knew Taj was right, but he couldn't resist adding, "I want them to put little flame emojis on either side of our names to show how we always kept it nice and warm."

Taj stifled a laugh and moved away from Marcus to keep out of trouble. But jokes aside, Marcus couldn't help wishing for a chance to get in the last game and shine. He was seriously going to hustle today.

2

After practice, on his way out of the gym, Marcus ran into Simone and her friend Olivia by the senior lockers. Simone was the starting forward on the girls' basketball team. He and Simone had grown up on the same street, shooting hoops together after school.

"Hey, Marcus," Simone said. "So, did you choke again? Or did you finally show Coach your moves?"

"I mean, I don't want to brag . . ."

Actually, he didn't want to talk about it at all. Marcus was tight with Simone, but he didn't feel comfortable around Olivia. He didn't know her that well . . . and she was really cute. Plus, he had nothing good to say. Practice had been a disaster. Julio had beaten him every time in the ball-handling matchups, and Marcus's team had been flattened in the scrimmage.

"You better get home. Your mom and dad are going to flip if you're late from practice again." Simone knew his family so well she was practically an honorary cousin. She lived down the street from him and had spent a million afternoons in their apartment courtyard, beating him at H-O-R-S-E.

"I know, I know," Marcus said. "Same as always."

At home, his dad was pulling together a salad, and his mom was pushing chicken cutlets around the pan, keeping one eye on the clock. She taught a weekly night class at the community college for English-language learners.

"There you are," she said. "Can you take over here? I've got to leave in, like, fifteen minutes and I haven't even printed out my notes."

"You don't need notes, Mom. You know this stuff cold. You should just riff." Marcus kissed her on the cheek and squeezed past her to the fridge to get some orange juice.

"Very sweet. But I prefer to come prepared. Now get over here and stir. And add those bell peppers for me." She put the spatula in his hand and went down the hallway, calling behind her, "You're a smart kid, Marcus. If you put as much extra time into your homework as you do into basketball, maybe you could get an academic scholarship."

His dad raised his eyebrows and nodded.

Not this again, Marcus thought, rolling his eyes. Both of them were obsessed with Marcus getting a good education—and that meant getting a scholarship. Second semester of senior year was a little late for that, but that didn't seem to stop his parents. Marcus scraped the chopped peppers into the pan and stirred.

His mom emerged from the bedroom, clutching her printouts. She grabbed her bag and keys. "Be good. I'll be back late."

His dad passed him a plate. "Eat. Then you can spend some time on that scholarship essay."

* * *

After wolfing down his dinner and washing up his dishes, Marcus grabbed a half-empty pint of ice cream and retreated to his bedroom. He opened his laptop to the scholarship application form, spooning mint chocolate chip into his mouth while he stared at the prompt:

> Discuss an accomplishment, event, or realization that sparked a new understanding of yourself or others.

What kind of question was that? He couldn't think of a single thing to write. Marcus grabbed a basketball and bounced it off the wall above his desk. His posters and photos fluttered, and the window frames rattled with each impact.

"Hey!" his dad called from the living room.

"Sorry!"

Marcus switched to practicing his jump

shot form, flicking the ball up and catching it repeatedly. His form was perfect when nobody was watching. Not that it did him any good. Marcus watched the ball spin up and backward, his middle finger the last one to touch it every time.

He grabbed the basketball to his stomach, already defeated, and texted Taj a string of emojis: basketball, trees, sunset. In other words: *Hey, wanna meet up and play a little one-on-one? Meet you at the park.* Marcus left the lights and music on in his room and the laptop open. He slipped past the living room, sneaking a peek from the hallway. Sure enough, his dad was falling asleep in front of the TV again. Marcus figured he'd probably have at least an hour before his dad woke up and came to check on him.

He eased the front door shut as quietly as possible behind him.

* * *

The wind picked up and Marcus pulled his hoodie closer around his neck. He should've grabbed a heavier coat, but he hadn't wanted to risk rustling in the coat closet and waking up his dad. March had been one of those long bitter months where he kept thinking maybe spring was almost here, but then the cold settled in even deeper.

He knew he'd warm up as soon as he started playing, though. He dribbled the ball from hand to hand, working on his ball handling. Then he forced himself to dribble with his left hand the rest of the way to the park. It only got away from him once or twice.

As he got closer to the court, he picked up his pace, dribbling the ball between his legs. It felt good to be outside, not stuck at his desk staring at that stupid essay question.

He stepped into the pool of light cast by the street lamp and sank a beautiful jump shot from way outside the line.

"Three points!" Taj emerged from the darkness and made crowd-goes-wild noises into his cupped hands. "Why didn't you sink them like that in practice today?"

Marcus grabbed the rebound and bounced it over to Taj. "I don't know, man. I just get choked up when I know people are watching."

"That's kind of a problem, dude. I've heard that people like to watch basketball."

Marcus rolled his eyes at him and slapped at the ball, getting in his space. "Come on, think you can get past me?"

"I know I can." Taj faked hard to his left, then tried to cut to the right.

But Marcus stayed on him tight. They'd been playing together so long, he knew all of Taj's moves. It was weird to think that they'd be going in different directions next fall. Taj was going out east to school. He'd gotten into some liberal arts college that his parents were all excited about.

Marcus was staying in town. He'd gotten accepted to the state university, but the hard truth was that without a scholarship, he wouldn't even be able to go there. He'd probably wind up at his mom's community college, where they could use her staff tuition benefit.

Taj muscled past him and jump stopped about three feet from the basket. He pulled up short, faked a shot, and then sank a power layup.

"Aw, man," Marcus said. "Nice shot." Taj grabbed the rebound and bounce passed it back to him.

"Come on," he said. "Let's play."

For right now, it felt good just to play one-on-one with his best friend.

* * *

In the morning, his mom asked him, "How are you doing on that scholarship essay?"

"Great," Marcus lied. "I'm almost done with my draft."

She beamed and hugged him. He didn't like to lie to her, but this one made her so happy. There was no way he could tell her that he was totally stuck—then all she'd do was worry more. "Good luck at the big game tonight, sweetie," his mom said. "I wish we could be there, but I've got another class, and your dad's got a night shift."

"That's okay, Mom, I'm probably not even going to play." Marcus grabbed a sweet bun from the box on the counter and went to the fridge to look for orange juice.

"Tell Simone to get video for me, okay?"

"You know she will." He gave her a kiss on the cheek, grabbed his backpack, and headed out the door.

* * *

All day long, Marcus was queasy with excitement. The whole school was decked out with signs and blue and gold balloons. It almost made the old place look good. Somebody had created a huge banner that hung over the front entrance. In huge letters, it said, "Go Wolves! Beat the Panthers!" On the left side of the banner, a cartoon wolf pack howled into the air. They were even wearing blue and gold jerseys. On the right side, they'd drawn a couple of cowardly panthers, tucking their tails under their butts and running away. *Man, somebody spent a lot of time on this*, Marcus thought.

Inside the hallways, every player's locker had good-luck notes taped to it along with paper flowers in the team's colors. This school had serious basketball fever. It felt good to be part of it, even if he was probably just going to ride the pine the whole game.

Simone bumped into him in the hallway and thumped him on the shoulder. "Hey, good luck! I'll be in the stands yelling for you guys."

"Thanks," Marcus said. He thumped her back. "Oh, hey, can you get some videos tonight for my mom? She and my dad can't make it."

"Working again, huh? Well, don't worry, you know I'll be getting footage." She disappeared into the crowd, trying to get to her class.

Marcus called out to her retreating back, "I'll just be on the bench, but try to get my good side."

Simone was the highest scorer on the girls' team—she didn't know what it was like to fail at your favorite sport.

3

The crowd drummed their feet against the bleachers, slow at first, then faster and faster. Marcus could feel his heartbeat match the accelerating rhythm. The drumbeat traveled down the hall and found them in the locker room.

They were playing across town at the other team's school. Everything here was so new it made him nervous. On their way in, the long halls had gleamed with packed trophy cases. Taj nudged him as they passed a whole wall of framed National Merit Scholar photos.

Even the locker room was nice. The lockers actually locked.

Coach Hunter gave them a quick pep talk before the game in the shiny new locker room. "Look, everyone knows this is a team you can't back down from. They expect to win this game, and they're not easy to rattle. They've got a strong defensive game, and that one big guy in the middle." Marcus remembered. They'd played them earlier this season, at home. The Wolves had lost, but at least they'd kept it close.

Coach Hunter freshened up his gum and went on, "But we can find the holes in their defense. Just keep moving the ball around, and I know we can wear them down. We're going to run them ragged, right? Tire them out! Keep your head up, stay aware of your teammates, and let Julio call the plays. Let's go get them!"

Even though it was technically an away game, the crowd in the gym was pretty evenly divided: half Wolves, half Panthers. One side of the bleachers was the familiar blue and gold, the other was a sea of maroon. It was cool but kind of nerve-racking. It felt like the entire student body of Booker T. Washington had come across town to cheer them on.

"Man, this gym is sweet," Taj muttered.

The Panthers' gym was state of the art. They had one of those giant, multi-angled scoreboards that was mounted on the ceiling, with video displays showing ads from local sponsors. It even showed player stats like the number of fouls. The bleachers were solid, not rickety, and there was actual space around the court for sidelines. At the Booker T. gym, people practically had to walk on the court to get to the concession stand.

As they started their warm-up drills, Marcus scanned the stands, trying to spot Simone. It didn't take long to find her.

She and Olivia were standing at the very top of the bleachers, holding up the same huge banner that Marcus had last seen hanging over Booker T. Washington's front entrance. The one with the crazy cartoons. Simone spotted him looking up and waved her free arm wildly, pointing at the sign in triumph. She was dressed from head to toe in blue and gold, and even her braids had school spirit—she had woven blue and gold ribbons into her hair.

Marcus shook his head and nudged Taj to take a look. "Did she steal that sign just to cheer us on?"

Taj looked up, then back at Marcus. "Of course she did." They did their signature handshake—dap, double-slap, finger-hook, hand explosion, chest bump—and then took their spots on the floor.

The cheerleaders lined up in two long rows alongside the team, and the announcer began calling out the names of the Wolves' starting lineup. Each player trotted through the corridor of teammates, giving low fives as they went, and then greeted their team manager at the end with a signature handshake.

Marcus wished that was him, doing his signature handshake as the announcer called out his name.

Instead, he and Taj took their seats on the sidelines, ready to follow the game and cheer on the team. But first the other side had their introductions. Marcus shook his head at the size of some of their players. They were even bigger than he remembered. He thought they were supposed to be a young team, but they looked like college students! He leaned over to Taj and whispered, "What are they feeding these guys?"

Taj said, "Oh, you know. The bones of their enemies."

The ref blew the whistle and tossed the ball in the air.

Zac tipped it to Julio, and the announcer called out, "Washington Wolves win the jump ball! And we're off. The Wolves have something to prove tonight. They're gunning for redemption. Booker T. lost narrowly to the Panthers in their last matchup, but it was a close one. Can they pull it off tonight?"

"Jeez, no pressure," Marcus muttered to Taj.

The game got off to a pretty good start. The Panthers were known for shutting down other teams by running an aggressive defensive zone, but Julio had a knack for finding the holes in it. He and Tyler broke up the full-court press like it was nothing, trading passes that always connected, zipping the ball down the floor. Marcus tried to study their technique.

And Zac kept finding ways to get open in the key. Julio bounce passed the ball over to Tyler, who popped it down to Zac, who muscled into the paint and sank it. The Panthers were making them work for it, but by the time the halftime buzzer blared, the Wolves' were leading by 16 points. The Wolves' side of the bleachers was going wild.

Taj leaned toward Marcus and yelled over the crowd, "This is amazing. We could totally make it to Districts!"

The Wolves all filed into the fancy, clean locker rooms and took a seat. But nobody could sit still. The energy was electric. Coach Hunter tried to look serious, narrowing his eyes at everybody to get them to settle down. But he couldn't totally keep the smile off his face. He wasn't even chewing his gum that hard. "All right, men, all right. Nice work out there. You're moving the ball really well. You've just got to keep running your plays, finding those openings, wearing them down. Good hustle under the basket, Zac. Everybody keep your eyes on Julio, and let him call the plays. I think we can do this—"

The whole team erupted into shouts and chest bumps.

Coach cut them off, "—*if* you stay focused. Now get some water, stay loose, and let's finish them off."

As the team milled around, Coach Hunter beckoned Marcus and Taj to come talk to him.

"Listen, I've seen how hard you two have been working in practice. Think you're ready to see some playing time?"

Marcus could feel his whole body tense up. He pressed his lips tightly together. He could barely breathe. He just quickly nodded three times.

Taj said, "Yes, sir. Definitely."

"All right, stay focused. I can't make any promises, but with a nice lead like this, I like to get seniors into the game. Marcus, you've really been showing a lot of fire in practice.

I know you think I only notice when you're goofing off," Coach raised an eyebrow and held his gaze, "but I see everything. And that's what you've got to do on the court. Remember that!"

Marcus held it together until Coach Hunter turned away. But the second the coach walked out of the locker room, Marcus collapsed in a dramatic heap on that squeaky-clean locker room floor. "Dude, we're going to playyyyyyy!"

Taj pulled him up, laughing, and said, "Hey, it hasn't happened yet."

"Yeah, but . . . it *could*." Marcus and Taj did an extended version of their handshake. Marcus couldn't help hopping with glee. He pulled himself together and followed the team back out into the gym.

The Panthers kept up the pressure in the second half, but the Wolves maintained a lead of around ten to twelve points. Marcus could hardly concentrate on the game, wondering if he was actually going to get a chance to play. He had a buzzing feeling in his head, like things were going to be different tonight.

And then in the final quarter, Coach Hunter leaned over and looked all the way down the bench. He beckoned to Taj. "Taj, come on. I'm putting you in." Marcus slapped him on the back, and looked at Coach expectantly. But Coach Hunter just turned away to talk to the ref about something.

Taj leapt up and ran over to give his number to the official. Coach Hunter called Zac out of the game to give him a chance to rest.

Marcus was happy for Taj, but he couldn't help feeling a pang of jealousy. What about his opportunity to play? He was a senior too. How cool would that be if they got to play together for maybe the last game of their entire high school career? He tried to replay the conversation with Coach from the locker room. He'd been pretty encouraging, right?

Realistically, Marcus knew it was going to be a different calculation for Coach Hunter, pulling another starter out of the game. He knew how important the starters were to keeping the lead. So Marcus settled into his cushy seat on the sidelines. He yelled really loudly every time Taj got his hands on the ball, no matter how briefly.

And then he saw it happen. Julio popped off a three-pointer but took a hard elbow in the ribs as he was fading away. He landed crooked on his ankle and went down hard. He was rocking back and forth on the floor, grabbing at his leg. The ref near him noticed right away and stopped the game. The whole crowd hummed with worry. Both teams gathered around.

Coach Hunter ran out onto the court to check on Julio and then called over the team manager. Together, they helped lift him off the ground. Julio tested his ankle and winced. He tried to walk it off, then shook his head. "I can't put any weight on it."

"Okay, let's get you taken care of." The two men slung Julio's arms over their shoulders and helped him walk off the court.

Everyone applauded with relief that he was walking. Well, hopping. It was pretty clear he had to sit out the rest of the game.

The team manager busied himself getting ice for Julio's ankle and finding an extra chair so they could keep his leg elevated. Coach Hunter turned to Marcus and crooked his finger at him. "Come on, Marcus. I'm putting you in."

Marcus froze and actually pointed at his own chest. "Me?"

"Yup. Tyler will take point. I want you in there as the shooting guard."

He was going *in*. He'd been on the bench the whole season, dreaming of this moment. This was exactly what he had always wanted, but not like this. He'd imagined playing with Julio, for one thing. Now he and Tyler would have to figure things out for themselves. And Julio left big shoes to fill. Tyler would have to lead the team, call all the plays, and keep everyone focused. But Marcus would have to step up too. He didn't want to let the team down.

Coach Hunter patted his pocket, checking for his gum, and said, "Come on, you've got this. I know you've got the skills, now you just need to deliver."

Marcus pushed to his feet and checked in with the ref. His coach gave him an encouraging nod, but Marcus thought he saw him chewing a little faster.

Taj ran over and gave him a high five. "Dude, you're in!"

Marcus tried to shrug casually. "Ha . . . yeah, guess so," he responded nervously.

Taj nodded. "Well, don't worry. The lead is so wide he probably figures even we can't blow it . . ."

They immediately started to blow it.

As soon as Marcus got his hands on the ball, he dribbled it off his foot, sending it out of bounds.

The opposing team inbounded the ball and set up an easy drive to the basket.

Coach Hunter smacked his clipboard and yelled, "Come on, get your head in the game, guys. You can do this!" He was chewing his gum so fast Marcus thought it was going to fly right out of his mouth.

Without Julio, the guys made error after error, but the crowd was still with them. Marcus could see Simone cheering loudly, loyally from the stands. She had handed the banner off to a friend—Olivia—and was taking video on her phone. Olivia was still cheering too.

Taj called over, "Just pretend we're in the park and nobody's watching."

Marcus nodded. *Sure. Just ignore reality! No problem.* But he tried to get his head into that space. Tried to channel that feeling of just having fun on the playground, shooting hoops with his best friend.

Tyler passed him the ball. Marcus popped up a jump shot and . . . *swish*.

The crowd went insane. Marcus looked around and caught Simone's eye in the crowd. She was yelling, "Yes, Marcus!" at the top of her lungs. Marcus looked at his feet, but he couldn't help smiling.

He just hoped they could hang onto the lead. It was narrowing by the minute, as their turnovers and missed shots accumulated. Julio cheered them on from the bench, but he looked nervous. The score was uncomfortably close.

Coach Hunter put their starting center Zac back in to give one of the other starters a break.

Taj was under the hoop, trying to get free from the other team's power forward, but the guy was a giant. He had six inches of height on Taj and easily fifty pounds. It was almost funny to watch Taj trying to box him out, but Marcus knew he had taken Coach Hunter's instructions to heart: "The more rebounds you grab, the more chances you get to score." Tyler put up a shot. No good. It bounced off the rim.

"Get in there, Taj," Coach shouted. "Box him out!"

Taj threw himself into the scuffle for the rebound and actually got his hands on it. Marcus shouted, "Yes, Taj!"

But then the big guy snatched it out of his hands like it was nothing and lobbed it down the court to the Panthers' fastest guard, who was wide open. They made good on the fast break and scored.

Taj looked like he was about to puke. Marcus could tell he was kicking himself for messing up that rebound. He couldn't bear to look over at Coach.

Now the game was tied up with less than a minute left on the clock. Taj held his head in his hands. He looked miserable. Marcus had always dreamed of getting to play in an actual game with his best friend, but now it felt more like a nightmare.

Coach Hunter looked nervous too, but he pulled them over for a quick time-out. "All right, listen. Do not give up the fight. This is *not* our last game of the season. I still think we can put this team away. Marcus, I want you to bring the ball down the court this time. Don't let them rattle you, okay? If you feel like you've got an opening, take the three-pointer."

Marcus felt his eyebrows go up. "You want me to take the shot?"

Coach Hunter said, "If you're open? Absolutely. I think they're underestimating you because they haven't seen much of your play. But I've seen you shooting around after practice. I've seen you sink those three-pointers. I know you can do it, if they leave you a window. And if you're not open, dish off to Taj and he'll draw the foul. That big guy has been on him all game." He patted Marcus on the back. "Come on, I believe in you guys!"

Marcus just had to get through the final seconds without totally screwing up. He had two good options. Coach believed in him. He just had to deliver.

Tyler inbounded the ball to Marcus. He started dribbling it down the court. The other team fell back into their zone, waiting for him to run the play. It was embarrassing how much space they were giving him. They clearly didn't see him as any kind of threat.

And that was his opportunity. He could make the three-point shot as long as he had some space to take it.

But Marcus hesitated as he crossed the half-court line. Could he actually make the shot? If he missed in front of the whole school, it would be so embarrassing. Should he dish off to Taj after all? He slowed down, dribbling the ball toward the top of the key, and the other team's defenders closed in around him. Two players, three. It felt like a wall of maroon jerseys. He couldn't see over them. A hand swatted at the ball. In a panic, he stopped dribbling and grabbed the ball to his stomach.

Now he was stuck.

4

Marcus clutched the ball and tried to pivot away from his defenders. He could feel his panic rising. He had three Panthers all up in his face, hands grabbing at him, a wall of maroon and white. He couldn't see any of his teammates, but he knew he couldn't let the Panthers just take the ball away. The fancy shot clock was ticking down the seconds. He had to do something. Anything. He couldn't dribble anymore, so he had to find a pass.

He heard Taj's voice sail over the crowd. "Come on, Marcus! You got this."

In desperation, he tried a scoop pass through the wall of defenders to Tyler, but a roar went up from the crowd. He had thrown it right into one of the Panther's arms instead. *No!*

And just like that, the other team was off on another fast break. Marcus was still reeling, and Tyler was struggling to get free of his defenders. Taj hustled back on defense. He was pounding down the court, coming up right behind the guard who had the ball.

The Panther guard tried to pass the ball to his teammate under the basket, but Taj bolted in between them and grabbed it off the bounce! He swerved to the right, leaving his defenders in the dust as he headed back up the court.

Marcus couldn't believe what he was seeing. He fell back on offense to help clear a path for Taj.

Taj drove hard to the basket. He was coming in a little out of control. Marcus followed, trying to get himself in position to catch the rebound if necessary. But Taj pulled up short and let the Panther defender go flying past him. Then he popped up a power layup, soft as butter, and it rolled right in off the backboard.

The buzzer blared. The game was over. They'd won!

The Wolves came streaming off the bench and dove on top of Taj in a happy pile.

Marcus could barely hear. The auditorium was thundering with foot stomps and shouts. The crowd was a blur of deliriously happy faces and pumping arms. The announcer was shouting, "Taj Reddy with a buzzer-beater, and the Wolves upset the Panthers! They are going to Districts!"

Marcus made his way over to Taj and gave him a pat on the back. He muttered, "Hey, you saved the day, man. Amazing play."

But he couldn't shake the embarrassment over his moment of panic. He felt like nobody could stand to look at him. They only had eyes for Taj. He got in line with the team for the postgame ritual of giving the opposing team high fives, everybody telling each other, "Good game, good game." After they all shook hands, the entire Wolves team lifted Taj up onto their shoulders and paraded him around the gym. Marcus stepped off to the sidelines, watching.

The Wolves fans all streamed onto the court, whooping and cheering. Somebody had grabbed the big banner and brought it down onto the floor. The team crashed through it on their second lap around the gym and then grabbed pieces of it to rip into confetti.

The coach called it off, finally. He had to whistle twice to get their attention. He brought them into a huddle for a quick pep talk before letting them go wash up. "That was great teamwork, you guys. Good job having each other's backs. I'm really proud of all of you, especially those of you who came in off the bench. Now let's not let it get quite that close next time . . ."

Blah, blah, blah. Marcus wasn't paying attention. All he could think about was what he assumed the coach was really thinking: *You let us down, Marcus.* He had choked.

He drifted away from the huddle. Everybody was still giving Taj high fives and trying to take selfies with him.

Simone came up to Marcus and tugged at his sleeve. "Hey, congratulations! You guys are going to Districts!"

"Mm-hmm."

"And you *played*."

Marcus grimaced. "Don't remind me."

Simone gave him a hard look. "Don't be like that. You guys won. And you scored, Marcus! Listen, I'll send you the photos—I got some good shots of you and Taj. It's so cool you guys got to play together!"

Marcus just nodded his head as she darted off to find Olivia.

Taj called over, "Hey, the team's going out for pizza to celebrate!"

Marcus looked at his shoes. "Yeah, I've got to head home. My mom's been on me about finishing that scholarship application." He turned on his heels and left.

* * *

But back in his bedroom, he couldn't think of a single word to write. He couldn't concentrate. Instead he was lying on his bed, tormenting himself by replaying the video snippets that Simone had sent him.

He stared at his phone screen, watching as he grabbed the ball up and immediately got swarmed by the other team. He hit pause so he wouldn't have to watch the next part. The part where he totally panicked and threw the ball away.

He lay face down on his bed, head buried in his pillow, and tried to press pause on his memories too. But the same stupid scene kept replaying in his brain.

His phone buzzed. Marcus rolled over and squinted at it. *What now?* A notification showed up on top of the paused video.

The message was from an unknown number:

Reply with YES for a free do-over.

Free do-over of what? He quickly typed a text to Simone.

What's up? Are you messing with me?

A couple minutes later, she texted back.

Huh?

Feeling stupid, he wrote back:

Never mind.

He should have known she wouldn't
do that.

But what kind of scam was this? Was
somebody from the other school messing
with him? Marcus googled the unknown
number, but he couldn't find any info online.
He texted Taj:

Hey, did you just text me from someone
else's phone?

He could see that Taj was writing a reply,
and then it finally appeared.

No, but did you change your mind? Want
a ride?

Nah. Thanks.

Out celebrating was the last place he wanted to be.

He heard the front door open. The sound of his mom's purse hitting the floor. Heavy shoes being kicked off. Dad must have picked her up after her class. He heard murmurs from the living room, and then his dad called down the hall, "Hey, Marcus, how'd the game go?"

He yelled back, "I'm working on my essay. Isn't that what you wanted?"

Marcus slammed his door shut, then bounced his basketball off the wall, hard.

"Hey!" his dad shouted, warning him to cut it out.

Marcus exhaled hard and then threw the basketball into the pile of dirty clothes in the corner. He went to the bathroom to brush his teeth and get ready for bed. He couldn't stop thinking about the game, though, and the idea of getting a do-over. If only that were possible. A chance to go back to that one horrible moment and do everything differently. He washed his face and shook his hands dry.

As he settled into bed, he rolled over, grabbed his phone off the nightstand, and read the message again. Before he turned off the light, he tapped a reply to the mysterious number.

YES.

5

Marcus woke up the next morning feeling groggy. He'd barely slept all night. Just tossed and turned, thinking about the game and how it went wrong. How he'd panicked and thrown the ball right to the other team when his own team needed him most.

When his alarm finally went off, he just lay there, willing himself to get up. He was dreading going to school today. There was going to be some big school assembly for the team. Marcus briefly considered pretending to be sick, but then he thought about Taj's buzzer-beater and decided he'd better toughen up. He'd go, and when they called out his friend's name, he'd cheer the loudest of anybody.

He rolled over and checked his phone. Weird—there was no record of the strange text exchange from last night.

No sign of his texts with Taj or Simone, either. All the photos and videos she'd sent him had been wiped out. He sat up in bed, wondering what had happened. His phone must have glitched.

Well, maybe that was for the best. Now he wouldn't be able to torment himself with the footage of the moment when he choked. If only he could wipe out the memories that kept running through his head too. And everybody else's.

He trudged down the hall to the kitchen and grabbed a bowl for cereal. His mom was pouring herself some coffee. Without looking up, she asked, "How are you doing on that scholarship essay?"

Marcus slammed the cereal box on the counter. "Can you stop with the nagging? You don't even care about how I played last night. I *sucked*, Mom. And now I have to go to school and face everybody."

"Hey!" She put the coffee mug down and turned to face him. "I'm sorry you had a bad practice. But you don't get to blow up at me." She poured in some sugar and stirred furiously. "Before I've even had my coffee. One bad scrimmage is not the end of the world, Marcus. Don't act like we didn't have an agreement about this already. You know we agreed that you were going to finish a first draft of that essay before the big game."

Marcus dropped into a chair at the kitchen table. *Before the big game? What is she talking about?*

Marcus was a realist. He knew it was most likely that his mom had gotten her dates messed up. That would make sense. A lot more sense than receiving a mysterious do-over from the void. In the cold light of day it seemed obvious that was wishful thinking.

Still, he had to check the date. He felt for his phone in his hoodie pocket.

His mom saw the look on his face and softened. "Hey, maybe it will be like when you have a terrible dress rehearsal. Isn't that supposed to be good luck for opening night? Anyway, good luck at the big game tonight. I wish I could be there, but I've got that night class and I couldn't find a sub."

Okay, this was definitely weird. His mom wouldn't forget that her weekly night class had been *last* night. He sneaked a look at the calendar on his phone. His phone thought it was yesterday again. But it could just be broken.

He decided not to say anything. He'd take his phone back to the store and see if they could help reset it. But he kept thinking back to that weird text message. Could it actually be happening?

His dad stumbled in and went straight for the coffee. "Hey, you were out late last night." He rubbed Marcus's head. "Back at the park for more practice with Taj?"

Marcus ducked away, his eyes wide. His dad laughed. "You think we don't notice?

I may be tired at the end of the day, but I'm not stupid."

But that wasn't what was freaking him out. He'd been at the park with Taj the night *before* last.

6

As he walked up to the main entrance of school, Marcus spotted something that stopped him cold. He craned his neck up to stare. The giant banner wishing the team luck was back over the front entrance, perfectly intact.

"Go Wolves! Beat the Panthers!" It had the exact same cartoon drawings of the howling wolf pack and the cowardly panthers running away.

Marcus squinted, looking for any signs of wear and tear. Not even a wrinkle, let alone a rip. The team had torn that thing into confetti last night.

A *do-over*. Impossible. But Marcus couldn't

deny the evidence that was hanging right in front of his eyes.

His wish had been granted. He was going to get a chance to change that moment when he'd choked, a chance to actually take the shot. He felt a shiver of excitement run all down his limbs, and he pulled his hoodie tighter.

"Pretty impressive, right?" Some kid Marcus barely knew had noticed him standing there, staring.

"Um, yeah, it's really good," he replied.

"Good luck at the game tonight," the kid said and headed into school.

Inside, everyone was wearing blue and gold, abuzz with excitement for the game that hadn't happened yet. The lockers had the exact same signs and paper flowers on them. Marcus felt like a time traveler. Was he the only one who knew they'd done all this before?

Marcus spotted Simone in the hallway. He grabbed her arm and pulled her off to the side. "Hey, are you coming to the game tonight?" He watched her face closely, trying to figure out if she knew what was happening.

She looked at him like he was nuts. "Marcus. Of course I'm going. The whole school's going. Hey, you should look for me and Olivia in the stands, we've got a little surprise planned."

He smiled. "Cool. Hey, listen, make sure to get a good seat. I have this weird feeling that I'm going to get to play tonight."

Her face lit up in surprise. "Okay—I'll get video if you do." She punched him in the arm and said, "Good luck!" Then she jogged away to catch up with Olivia.

Marcus couldn't stop smiling. He drummed a quick beat on his locker door, and then headed off to Spanish class. He was going to kill it on the quiz today. He knew exactly which questions he'd gotten wrong last time.

* * *

That night, the ref blew his whistle and tossed the ball in the air.

The crowd drummed their feet against the bleachers, slow at first, then faster and faster. The Wolves won the jump ball again.

Marcus looked around, trying to take it all in this time. The first time through had been a blur. And frankly, he'd kind of checked out, since it had seemed so unlikely that he would ever get a chance to play. This time, he'd be ready.

He tried to figure out how Julio did it, spotting the open players so easily, always in control of the ball. He studied each play, trying to figure out the Panthers' strengths and weaknesses. Marcus couldn't stop his knees from bouncing with excitement. He couldn't wait to get back in the game.

The Wolves opened up a nice lead, just like before. Coach Hunter gave them the exact same pep talk at halftime, in the shiny, clean locker room. Just like before, Taj subbed in for Zac. And then it happened again: Julio came down hard and twisted his ankle.

It looked so painful. Marcus winced in sympathy as Julio rocked back and forth, clutching his leg. It suddenly struck him that he should have warned him somehow. He'd been so focused on how he'd choked in the final moments of the game, he had sort of forgotten how he'd wound up playing. He wondered if he should have said something. Could he have warned Coach Hunter that Julio's defender was checking him too hard? Told Julio to be careful? But how would he have possibly convinced anyone? He couldn't have explained that he'd lived through all this before. It was too bizarre to believe.

The coach and team manager helped Julio limp off the court.

Coach Hunter waved Marcus over.

Marcus jumped up with zero hesitation. *Yes.* This time he was ready. He knew what he had to do.

Taj ran over and gave him a high five. "Dude, you're in!"

Marcus laughed. "Yeah. Let's do this."

But despite his best efforts, the other team started to close in on their lead, just like last time. Marcus tried to change things around, but he kept making the same stupid mistakes as before. Botched passes, missed shots. Taj was clearly nervous too. Marcus could see it on his face—Taj was struggling to keep up with that giant under the basket. He tried to box him out, but it was like trying to budge a mountain.

The fancy video scoreboard was ticking down the seconds. The Wolves put up a shot, but nothing was sinking for them. Taj tried to get in position to grab the rebound, but he just didn't have the reach. He almost got his hands on the ball, but then the giant swatted it away again and tossed it down the court. The Panther guard caught the lob and took it up for an easy layup. The Panther side of the gym went crazy with excitement. Suddenly they were tied up, with less than a minute to go.

Coach Hunter called for a time-out and waved them all over. His jaw was going a mile a minute on that gum. Taj held his head in his hands. He was kicking himself for missing that rebound.

Marcus felt like he was trapped in a bad dream. *What good is a do-over if I let it all play out the same way?* Marcus whispered to himself, "Dude, concentrate. You have to change your fate."

Coach Hunter gave him a weird look, then snapped his fingers in front of Marcus's face to get his attention.

"All right, listen," Coach said. "Do not give up the fight. I still think we can put this game away. Marcus, I want you to bring the ball down the court. Don't let them rattle you, okay? If you feel like they're closing in, dish off to Taj so he can draw the foul."

"Coach, I can do this." Marcus could see the coach hesitate. "I promise I won't let you down. I'll come through, I swear."

Coach blinked in surprise. "I know that you will."

The refs blew the whistle. The game was back on.

Tyler took the ball on the sideline and was about to inbound it to Marcus.

This was it. His last chance to turn things around. Marcus took a deep breath. *Don't choke. Don't freeze.*

He looked at Tyler and said, "Stay with me, okay, just in case I get trapped?"

Tyler nodded and passed the ball to Marcus,

then trotted along next to him. Marcus could hear Taj yelling, "Let's go, Marcus. You've got this!"

Marcus scanned the court. He could see that the Panthers had fallen back into a loose zone, waiting for him to get a little closer to make their move. He realized his coach was right. He was open. He could take advantage of his defenders underestimating him.

This time he didn't hesitate. Marcus took a deep breath to keep his nerves in check. He kept his dribble low and controlled as he crossed the half-court line. Tyler was staying close by, but Marcus felt like he had it under control. He sensed exactly when they started to move in on him.

He could see Taj under the basket, jockeying for position with his defender. He caught Marcus's eye and clapped his hands for the ball. But Marcus could barely see him through the big guy's waving arms. He wasn't convinced Taj could actually get open for a pass. The last thing he wanted to do was throw the ball away again.

Marcus nodded to Taj as if to signal he was about to pass.

He dribbled a little closer then cut hard to the left, pulled up short, and surprised them with a nice soft jump shot from way outside the three-point line. *Oh please, oh please, go in.*

It felt good leaving his hands, but it was a long shot. Everyone under the basket turned to watch its arc, ready to box out for that rebound.

Taj got into position by the giant, ready to do his best.

Marcus froze, willing it to sink, hands still cocked in the air. It bounced hard on the rim, hit the backboard, and bobbled to the other side of the hoop. The entire gym seemed to hold its breath, unnaturally quiet, as the ball wobbled on the rim and rolled and rolled.

And then it fell in.

There was another second of silence as everyone processed what had just happened. And then the crowd exploded.

"Marcus Robertson, off the bench with a three!" The announcer was beside himself.

Marcus felt like his face was going to break,

his smile was so big. There were just seconds left on the clock. The Panthers grabbed the ball and heaved it inbounds, but it was too late. Too desperate. The pass didn't connect, the buzzer sounded, and the game was over. The Wolves had won!

And this time, it was Marcus who had saved the day.

The crowd went wild and stormed the court. The announcer shouted, "Marcus Robertson, out of nowhere! The Wolves have won their place at Districts!"

He let his teammates lift him up onto their shoulders, chanting and stomping. "Go, Wolves! Go, Wolves!" This time he was the one getting paraded around the gym. The gym was a blur of blue and gold and happy, chanting faces. The Wolves fans poured down the bleachers, and the players ran through the sign like last time, ripping it into pieces. Marcus slid off Tyler's shoulders and grabbed a piece of the sign as a souvenir—a nice big chunk that had one of the howling wolves on it. He waved it in the air.

Then he spotted Taj off to the side.

"Hey!" Marcus ran over to Taj. "We did it!"

"You did it, man. That was amazing." Taj gave him a quick high five, but it didn't seem like his heart was in it. He ducked away from Marcus to go get a drink.

Coach Hunter was shaking the other coach's hand, and he gave them a stern head bob, instructing them to get in line to shake hands too. Both teams filed past each other murmuring, "Good game, good game." A couple Panthers even said, "Hey, nice shot," as they passed Marcus.

Simone and Olivia came over, and Simone asked Taj and Marcus to pose together. Marcus slung his arm around Taj's neck and held his finger up in a number one sign with his other hand. Taj just pointed at Marcus's chest.

"Bro, smile." Simone said. "You're going to Districts!"

"Hope I don't embarrass myself there too," Taj muttered. "That big guy made me look like a punk."

"Hey, don't be like that," said Marcus.

"Does this crowd look like they're embarrassed by us?" He gestured around at all of their friends going nuts.

"No, good point. But the only reason we were tied up was because I missed that rebound right at the end of the game. That guy plucked it right out of my hands."

"But we still won! Come on, Taj, let's go get some pizza. The whole team is going out to celebrate."

But Taj shook his head. "I need to finish up my homework."

Marcus tilted his head. "Tonight? Come on, come out with us. Hey, listen, you could have made that shot. I'm just relieved I didn't mess it up."

Taj nodded. "Right. Like me, when I messed up the rebound."

"Man, that's not what I meant. You know that."

"No, I know you didn't, but come on. I was the turnover king all night long. After all those speeches Coach gave about the importance of rebounding and controlling possession of the ball." Taj looked miserable. "There's no way Coach is going to trust me to play again."

Marcus didn't know what to say. "I . . . listen, man. Be happy. We won! We're going to Districts!"

"Yeah." Taj headed for the locker room. "I'm going to go wash up. Have fun."

Marcus let Zac and Tyler pull him away for another selfie. He grabbed a ride with them over to Pizza Town. In the car, his phone kept buzzing with messages from Simone and Olivia and random classmates he barely knew. They were all texting him photos and video snippets that they'd taken of his big moment.

He was distracted, though, and felt kind of weird. People he didn't even know kept high-fiving him and buying him pizza. He wished Taj was there. It was unbelievable how much difference just a few seconds could make. Last night they had won the game too, but he had gone home completely miserable and Taj had been out with the team. He just hoped that Taj wasn't beating himself up with regrets the same way he had.

But then Simone and Olivia came in and all thoughts of Taj melted away. Olivia was so pretty. She waved and said, "Hey," and Marcus could feel his cheeks heating up.

Simone dragged her friend over and pulled some chairs up to the team's table. She nudged Marcus. "Hey, rock star! Off the benches and into the books! I'll admit it now, I thought you were bluffing this morning when you said you were going to see some playing time tonight."

He laughed awkwardly. "Well, you know. You're always telling me to trust my intuition. I just had a good feeling about it."

And it did feel good. Whenever Marcus thought about that ball leaving his hands and soaring through the air, he couldn't help but smile. He had finally proved he could rise to the challenge. He was glad he'd taken the shot and even more relieved that he'd actually made that basket. He'd never forget the amazing feeling when it fell through the net, and for a few seconds, an entire gym full of people forgot to breathe.

7

The next morning, Marcus didn't want to go to the kitchen for breakfast. He lay in bed replaying the last amazing seconds of the game in his head. The long arc of the ball through the air, the endless roll around the rim, the beautiful *swish* as it sank, at last.

The quiet. Then the roar.

He didn't even want to look at his phone. He was worried that the video snippets had disappeared again, that the whole beautiful moment had been a dream. He'd done it. He knew he had. But would anyone else remember?

He wondered if his mom was going to nag him about his college essay again when he walked in to get some breakfast. Would she wish him luck at the big game? Apologize for not being able to find a sub? Was he going to be stuck reliving this stupid stressful day forever?

But then he had a thought.

He leaped out of bed and kneeled on the carpet by his backpack. He unzipped it and rummaged around, holding his breath.

And then he found it. The scrap of the banner he'd grabbed last night as a trophy. The edges were torn and the paper was wrinkled from being shoved deep in his bag, but it was the most beautiful ripped-up thing he'd ever seen. It meant that whole magical night was real. He'd really done it. He had made that amazing three-point shot, and the whole school had cheered his name.

He took it over to his desk so he could carefully smooth it out. Then he tacked it up on his corkboard and stepped back to admire it.

He could barely tear himself away, but then he remembered that there was going to be a school assembly today for the team. He got dressed in a hurry and practically bounced down the hallway for breakfast.

His mom was wearing her pajamas and reading the paper at the kitchen table, like she always did on her day off from daytime classes. Marcus jumped up to slap the doorframe as he entered the kitchen, and she looked up from her coffee. "Hey, he lives! I picked up juice for you on the way home last night. I didn't even hear you come in, I was so beat. I've been dying to know, how did the big game go?"

Marcus grabbed a bowl from the cabinet and sauntered over to the fridge to grab some milk for his cereal. "Oh, it went pretty well." He shrugged. "I just scored the winning shot!"

"What! I thought you said you weren't going to play." His mom leapt up from the table and pulled him in for a hug. Then she held him out at arm's length so she could look at him. "Honey, that's amazing. I'm so proud of you."

Marcus ducked his head and grinned. "It was pretty cool, I'm not gonna lie."

His mom added, "You should work that into your scholarship essay! How perseverance and hard work pays off!"

Marcus pulled away. Why did she have to make everything about college? He muttered, "More like how one lucky break can turn you into a hero."

His mom rolled her eyes and sighed. "I can't even compliment you?"

"Mom, I can't right now." Marcus took his cereal with him as he went back to his room to finish getting ready for school.

* * *

Things got better the second he walked onto the school grounds. A freshman ran up to him and said, "Hey, you're Marcus Robertson, right? That shot was incredible! Can you sign my program?" He thrust the game program and a pen into Marcus's hands. Marcus signed it, feeling like a minor celebrity. The kid asked him, "Do you think we'll win at Districts?"

Marcus shrugged and said modestly, "We'll do our best."

It was like that all day. Marcus was getting extra attention at school from literally everyone. The cute girl in his Spanish class let him share her notes. A couple of the football players actually acknowledged him in the hallway. People who'd never spoken to him before recognized him in the halls and congratulated him on his shot. Everyone was pumped for the school assembly that afternoon.

His math teacher, Ms. Kendall, called him over as he came into class. Marcus assumed he was in trouble. He checked the clock over the doorway, wondering if he was late. But Ms. Kendall just shook his hand, in her very serious way, and said, "Congratulations. That was a beautiful parabola."

He blinked. "A what now?"

"The arc of your shot," she clarified, drawing a rainbow through the air with her finger. "Geometry is everywhere, Marcus! See, I told you that you could use math in real life. And even better when you can use it to beat the Panthers." She winked and nodded at him to take his seat.

Marcus could get used to this.

When the bell rang for the last period of the day, all the students filed into the school auditorium for the assembly. The team sat in the front couple rows, and the principal, Mrs. Watson, came onto the stage. She took the microphone to congratulate them on the big win and wish them luck at Districts. The whole school jumped up and gave a standing ovation. "And I know you'll all show that same good sportsmanship," she continued, "when you beat Lincoln at the District tournament! Now I think Coach Hunter has an announcement he'd like to make." She turned over the microphone to the coach.

Coach Hunter asked everybody to sit down for a second. "I want to acknowledge some major growth last night," he said. "We had a big setback when Julio got injured, but everybody really stepped up and contributed. First, can we please have a big round of applause for Julio? Thank you, Julio, for your leadership this whole season."

In the front row, Julio used one of his crutches to rise to his feet and turned around to wave to everybody.

Coach Hunter raised his arms and got everybody to quiet down again. He went on, "One player especially surprised me, though. That player rose to the occasion at a moment of extreme stress. When it really counted, this player seized the moment and came through for the team." Coach paused, smile lines crinkling up his face. He was clearly savoring the drama. "That's why I'm very pleased to announce that . . . Marcus Robertson is our most valuable player of the month!"

"Yeah! Marcus!" The whole school applauded, and his teammates shoved Marcus forward. Coach Hunter waved him up, so he ran up the steps to the stage and turned to face the crowd. He scanned the sea of faces, looking for his friends. He spotted Simone, behind her phone as always, and gave her a quick embarrassed nod. It was kind of cool that she was getting video, though. Maybe his parents would finally understand what a big deal this was when they saw footage of the whole school assembly.

Then Marcus spotted Taj. He was hanging at the edge of the team by himself. He was clapping, but he still looked kind of miserable. Marcus felt a twinge of guilt. But then he thought, *Why can't Taj just be happy for me?*

Coach Hunter presented Marcus with a big MVP ribbon and a gift certificate for Pizza Town. The whole school cheered wildly for him. It felt pretty great. He shook Coach's hand, then hopped off the stage to take his seat with the rest of the team again.

After the assembly, Coach pulled him aside.

"Marcus, I was impressed with the way you handled yourself in the game last night. That was a high-pressure situation, and you rose to the occasion. Not every player can handle a stressful situation like that and still deliver. Julio's going to be out for a while with the sprained ankle, so I'd like you to start in the next game."

Marcus gulped. "Really? Coach, I will not

let you down. This has been my dream for, like, forever."

"You'll do great." Coach Hunter laughed and smacked him on the shoulder. "Now give me a good practice today—show me that I'm making the right choice."

"Yes, sir!"

Marcus ran to find Taj. He caught up to him as he was leaving the auditorium and grabbed his sleeve. Taj whirled around and yanked his arm free. "What?" He didn't look directly at Marcus.

Marcus said, "Sorry, I just wanted to tell you . . ." He broke off. Now didn't seem like the best time to share his good news. "How are you doing?"

"I'm fine." Taj raised his eyebrows. "We done?"

"Come on, man. You're not still thinking about that rebound, are you? That dude was a giant. Coach knows you did everything you could."

"Oh, did he tell you that when he was giving you all the prizes? I guess he knows who his new star player is. Mr. MVP, who couldn't bear to pass the ball, even though I was totally open."

"Taj, I tried. That guy had you covered! You said it yourself, he was on you the whole game."

"You looked right at me, then you took the shot yourself!"

"Coach told me to! I was only supposed to pass if I couldn't make the shot. And I did make the shot, remember?"

"Yeah, I remember. Everyone is always going to remember who made the winning shot. Congratulations."

"Wow, thanks. Man, you're really sucking all of the joy out of this. I thought maybe you would be happy for me."

Taj sighed. "I know. I'm sorry. It's just . . . a lot. Listen, I'll see you at practice. I've got to go change."

"Okay."

Marcus thought back to how happy Taj was the first time they'd played against the Panthers, when he had been the one to make the winning shot. He had been able to redeem his own mistakes—and Marcus's. He had saved the day when Marcus messed up.

Marcus hated that fixing his big mistake had left Taj feeling like his own mistakes defined him. Now Taj felt like a loser—the way Marcus had before.

He had basically stolen Taj's moment of triumph to get his own. Now Taj would never know that he had actually made the winning shot the first time around. Not only the winning shot—he'd stolen the ball from the other team!

Marcus knew he had to make it up to him, but he had no idea how.

8

Marcus played hard in practice that afternoon, but he couldn't seem to find the sweet spot. During warm-up he kept trying his go-to, the three-pointer, but nothing was working. His shots kept clunking off the rim. And then he tried a baseline jumper that soared over the basket completely.

Tyler caught it on the other side. "Air ball!"

"What's up, superstar?" Taj said. "Lost your touch?"

Taj might have been teasing, but his words stung. Marcus glared at him but secretly worried that he was right. What if that was just a lucky shot the other night? He didn't want to let the team down—especially not at Districts.

Zac overheard the jab and shot back, "Hey, at least Marcus made the shot when it counted!"

"What are you saying?" Taj's grin vanished. "That I choked?"

"That's not what I—"

"You don't think I know that?"

Marcus tried to grab his arm to calm him down, but Taj shook him off and stormed away.

The rest of practice, it felt like nothing went right. Marcus couldn't seem to get the ball moving. Passes that looked totally open led to steals. It was like he had lost all sense of how long it actually took for the ball to get from his hands to another person's. Every time he thought someone was open, the other side would materialize out of thin air to steal the ball. Or the teammate that he thought was looking for his pass turned out to be moving away from the ball, and Marcus's pass went right out of bounds.

"Oh, come on! Stay alert," he yelled at Zac. Zac raised his eyebrows and just stood there looking at him. Marcus flinched and muttered, "Sorry." He ran to collect the ball himself.

As he came back down the court, he dribbled the ball hard and low, trying to get his emotions in check. He had to show Coach Hunter he could do this. But his passes just weren't connecting and it felt like even his shooting had gone cold. One time, Tyler stripped the ball away from him as he was dribbling it down the court. Tyler dished it down to Taj, who powered in for a layup.

Coach Hunter just watched quietly from the sidelines. He called out, "Use your pivot!" periodically, when he could see Marcus was feeling trapped. And "Talk to each other!" But he didn't seem super concerned.

Marcus could feel his anxiety rising. *What if I'm not ready to play at Districts?* he worried. He'd made one lucky shot, with the advantage of knowing exactly how the defenders were going to play against him. That didn't mean he knew how to read the court or call the plays.

He wished Julio hadn't gotten hurt. What made Coach think he was ready to start in the tournament? This could turn into a total disaster. He wanted to play, but he didn't want to let everybody down.

After practice, Marcus texted Simone:

Hey, need to talk to you. Meet me at Pizza Town?

* * *

Marcus spotted Simone in the back of the shop—she had already grabbed their usual booth. He waved the MVP gift certificate in the air. "Whatcha want? I'm buying!"

"Well, all right, big spender." Simone laughed. "One Sicilian slice for me. Pepperoni."

"Got it." Marcus ordered three slices and a couple of sodas.

"So, what's up?" Simone said as he slid into the booth across from her. The pepperoni smelled amazing. Marcus loved how the edges got all dark and crispy where the cheese hit the edge of the pan. He took a big bite to buy a little time.

How could he explain his dilemma without telling her about the do-over? He'd known Simone forever, but how could she possibly believe his story? He could barely believe it himself.

Marcus chewed, holding his finger up to show that he couldn't talk yet.

"Come on." Simone sipped her drink. "What was so urgent you had to send out the bat signal?"

"It's just . . ." Marcus struggled to figure out what he could safely say. "Coach asked me to start at our next game."

"Hey, congratulations!" Simone wadded up a napkin and tossed it at him. "See, I knew you could do it."

"Ha. Maybe you knew. I never did. Anyway, it's amazing, right? And I thought Taj would be happy for me. But now he's being a jerk. He's acting all mad at me. I can't help it that I played well and he didn't!"

Simone said, "Mm-hmm."

"What?" Marcus shifted in his seat.

"Is that really what's bothering you?" She leaned forward. "Taj gets in his feels sometimes. He'll get over it. Why can't you just give him some time?"

Marcus rolled his straw wrapper between both hands, then tied it into a knot. Then another. Then he tossed it onto the table. "Why does Coach Hunter think I can handle starting? I could barely make a basket all practice! I keep throwing passes to people who aren't open. What if that shot was a fluke?"

"And there it is," Simone said.

"There what is?"

"What you're really worried about. You're worried you're going to let down the team."

"It's not that . . ." Marcus pulled his straw out of his drink, then punched it back in. "I don't know. Maybe."

Simone put down her drink and grabbed his wrist. He stared at his wrist, and then back up at her, smirking.

"Are you trying to hold my hand?"

She rolled her eyes. "Listen to me, idiot.

You've got to be in it to win it. If the coach thinks you're ready, then you are. He's been watching you all season, not just that one game. Why do you think he always pairs you up against Julio in practice? He must think you guys have a similar style of play. Just get out of your head and give it your all. I know how many times you've been out late practicing in the park. Why don't you trust that you've actually learned something?"

She released his wrist and shook her head. "Actually, you and Taj are a lot alike. You both need to have a little more faith in your form. That shot didn't just come from nowhere—it's not magic, right? It's practice."

Marcus winced. It was sort of both, but how could he possibly explain?

Simone went on. "It's the same thing for being a starter. You just need a little more practice. Julio's not a wizard. He's just been playing in more game situations than you have. He's used to reading the court, knowing where everybody is. But I know you can do it. And you should be happy that Coach

Hunter sees your potential. He knows what he's doing."

"Yeah. Okay. Thanks." He sighed and slid out of the booth to leave. She didn't understand. The first Districts game was in two days. How was he going to develop his basketball IQ and passing game in two days?

"Marcus, wait." Simone looked serious. "I feel like there's something you aren't telling me."

"What . . ." He shook his head nervously.

"That's okay. You don't have to. But . . . just don't stay mad at Taj, okay? You guys have been friends for too long to let something stupid get between you. I know you can figure out how to make things right."

Marcus couldn't think of anything to say in response. He settled for giving her a quick nod before heading for the door. But he could feel her watching him as he scraped his garbage into the can, slid their empty tray onto the counter, and left.

Come on. It wasn't fair. How did she know so much?

9

At the next practice, Marcus really tried to focus. He kept his head up and his eyes on the other players.

They were working on passing drills today—first monkey in the middle, then pass and follow exercises like the four-corner drill. He dribbled to the middle of the square, jump stopped, pivoted, and passed to the person in the next corner. It was a relief to know exactly what to do and where he was supposed to be at all times. The constant motion of the ball gave him something to concentrate on. He had to keep up with the flow. No time to get lost in his thoughts. All he had to do was stay focused and keep up so he wouldn't get beaned in the head.

He was playing better than ever before, making sharper connections. But something still felt off.

Taj wasn't talking to him. He wasn't making snotty comments anymore, either. But Marcus missed talking smack with him during practice.

They finished up the drill, and then everybody lined up to get a drink of water. Marcus looked over and saw that Julio had come in to watch them practice. He had a big boot on, but at least he was walking. Maybe he'd have some tips for him. He watched as Julio moved his crutches under one arm and used them to lower himself carefully onto the bleachers next to Coach Hunter. Julio turned to prop his crutches upside down next to him. Coach Hunter patted him on the back. They leaned their heads together to talk.

Marcus knew he couldn't go back in time and prevent Julio from getting hurt. He could only move forward, but at least he could try to put one thing right. He dropped out of the line for water, then went over to Julio and the coach.

"Hey, Coach, can we talk?" Coach Hunter finished making a note on his clipboard, then looked up at Marcus. "Sure. Do you want to talk privately?"

Marcus looked at Julio and shook his head. "No, that's okay." He nodded at Julio. "Hey, man, how's your leg?"

Julio shrugged it off. "It'll be all right."

Marcus put his hands on his hips, staring at the floorboards. He was trying to get his thoughts in order before he started talking, but then it all came spilling out in a rush. "Listen, don't get me wrong, Coach, I was really excited to get the starting spot, but I think the whole team should have a chance. We all played really hard the other night. I made some stupid mistakes before I made that shot. Maybe there's . . . somebody else who could have produced too, if they'd been given the opportunity." He looked up and faced Coach squarely. "Can we scrimmage for the open starting spot at Districts?"

Coach Hunter looked him in the eye and chewed his gum very slowly. He said, "Are you second-guessing me?"

"I just want everyone to have a fair shot at starting," Marcus said.

He squinted at Marcus, then shook his head. "You're nervous. Don't be. You earned your spot, and you're going to do great. I need a guard, and you're a strong outside shooter."

Marcus was so tempted to say okay and leave it at that. He'd tried, right?

But then he thought of Taj—how excited he was when he had made the winning shot and how depressed he'd been when he'd lost his chance to correct his mistake.

Marcus took a deep breath and tried again. "Honestly, Coach, I think there are some other players on the team who have a lot of potential too. Can you just promise me that you'll have a scrimmage and take into account who's hustling the hardest? I know we made some mistakes in the last game, but we all played our hardest and we learned from it. And maybe if people knew there was a chance they'd get to play, they'd practice even harder."

Coach clapped him on the shoulder and said, "Marcus, I love how you're stepping up this year. I'm not making any promises, but we can shake things up a little."

Coach Hunter blew his whistle and called the team over. Everybody was excited to see Julio there and ran over to say hey.

Coach explained that they were going to do things a little differently this week. "Marcus here had a good idea. Usually things are pretty settled by this time in a season. But as we saw the other night, sometimes players can surprise you. So I'm not going to make any assumptions. You all played your hearts out the other night against the Panthers. If you can play like that in practice for the rest of the week, with that same level of intensity, I will make sure that every single one of you sees some playing time at Districts."

The whole team hollered with excitement. Taj looked stunned. He shot Marcus a questioning look, and Marcus just shrugged.

The coach blew a couple short, sharp blasts on his whistle to get everybody to settle down again. "So we're going to scrimmage again, you guys. Are you ready? Give it your all. Let's count off."

Marcus and Taj wound up on the same team this time. Taj elbowed him and said, "That was pretty cool of you to talk to Coach."

Marcus felt the glow he had been expecting to feel the other night, when he made the winning shot. He extended his fist and said, "Don't leave me hanging." Taj laughed and came in for an epic handshake.

Taj added, kind of low, "Hey, I'm sorry about making those cracks in practice the other day. I was out of line."

Marcus looked at his friend and then down the length of the court. "Dude, don't worry about it. Now let's show everybody that the benchwarmers came to play!" They both cracked up, and then the whistle shrilled and they were off.

10

Marcus opened up his laptop and read the prompt for his scholarship essay for the umpteenth time.

Discuss an accomplishment, event, or realization that sparked a new understanding of yourself or others.

Ugh. The essay was due by midnight tonight, and he still had zero idea what to say. He bounced his basketball off the wall over his desk, trying to switch hands each time.

"Hey!" his dad yelled down the hall. "More writing, less bouncing!"

"Sorry!"

He switched over to his phone and read the school blog's recap of the first District game. He had read it probably fourteen times already, and it never got old:

> The Wolves battled to an exciting win despite their star point guard's season-ending injury. The back bench rose to the challenge, and workhorses Marcus Robertson and Taj Reddy pulled off a game-changing fast break with just seconds on the clock to win their first District game.
>
> Robertson spotted Reddy open at the far end of the court and lobbed a perfect pass to set him up for the buzzer-beater. Coach Hunter credited his seniors' great attitude for the win. "Between Marcus's assist and Taj's power layup at the end of the game, they sealed the deal for us. I couldn't be prouder of how they showed up every day in practice, even when they weren't getting much game time, and worked together for this moment.

Marcus's phone buzzed, and he startled.

Not again.

But it was just a text from Taj asking to hang out: pizza slice emoji + question mark. Marcus exhaled and texted back.

Later! I've got something I need to finish first.

He turned his attention back to the screen. Then he typed:

What if you were given a chance at a do-over?